No Monsters Here

To Melanie Colbert, with gratitude
— Sharon

For Deb, who told me I came from Mars
— Ruth

Text copyright © 2004 by Sharon Jennings
Illustration copyright © 2004 by Ruth Ohi
First published in paperback in 2006.

In Canada
Fitzhenry & Whiteside Limited
195 Allstate Parkway
Markham, Ontario   L3R 4T8

www.fitzhenry.ca

In the United States
Fitzhenry & Whiteside Limited
311 Washington Street,
Brighton, Massachusetts 01235

godwit@fitzhenry.ca

10 9 8 7 6 5 4 3 2 1

National Library of Canada Cataloguing in Publication

Jennings, Sharon
        No monsters here / Sharon Jennings ; illustrations by Ruth Ohi.

For children aged 3-6.
ISBN 1-55041-787-8 (bound).—ISBN 1-55041-789-4 (pbk.)

I. Ohi, Ruth II. Title.

PS8569.E563N6 2004   jC813'.54   C2003-907364-5

Publisher Cataloging-in-Publication Data
(Library of Congress Standards)

Jennings, Sharon.
No monsters here / Sharon Jennings ; illustrations by Ruth Ohi.—1st ed.
[24] p. : col. ill. ; cm.
Summary: A brave little boy assures his timid father that there is nothing to fear in this role-reversal story where the monsters are more interested in cookies than giving anyone a real scare.
ISBN 1-55041-787-8
ISBN 1-55041-789-4 (pbk.)
1. Courage – Fiction – Juvenile literature. 2. Fathers and sons – Fiction – Juvenile literature. (1. Courage – Fiction. 2. Fathers and sons – Fiction.) I. Ohi, Ruth. II. Title.
[E] 21   PZ7. J466Nm 2004

Fitzhenry & Whiteside acknowledges with thanks the Canada Council for the Arts, and the Ontario Arts Council for their support of our publishing program. We acknowledge the financial support of the Government of Canada through the Book Publishing Industry Development Program (BPIDP) for our publishing activities.

Printed in Hong Kong

Design by Blair Kerrigan/Glyphics

No Monsters Here

Sharon Jennings • Ruth Ohi

Fitzhenry & Whiteside

My father does not want me to go to bed. He is afraid of monsters.

Every night, when it starts to get late, my father looks at the clock.

"I think that clock is broken," he says. "It isn't time for bed. You can stay up a bit longer."

"But I *want* to go to bed," I tell him. "I am very very tired."

My father takes me to the kitchen. "Would you like another cookie?" he asks.

"I have had enough cookies," I tell him. "I want to go to sleep."

We stand at the bottom
of the stairs. It is dark at the top.
My father sighs a very big sigh.

"I will hold your hand," I tell him.

At my bedroom door, my father asks,
"Wouldn't you like to sleep in my room tonight?"

"No," I say. "I like my own room best."

I turn on my light and look around. "You can come in now," I let my father know.

But he shakes his head. He is afraid of monsters.

"Look under the bed," my father says.

So I do. There's nothing there but toys.

"No monsters here," I tell him.

"Look in the closet," my father says.

So I do. There's nothing there but clothes.

"No monsters here," I tell him.

"Look behind the curtains," my father says.

So I do. There's nothing there but night.

"No monsters here," I tell him.

"Look under the covers," my father says.

So I do. There's nothing there but me.

"I am not a monster," I tell him.

My father takes giant steps to jump on my bed.

"Now we can read a story," I tell him.

"Don't pick a scary one," my father says.